PUFFIN BOOKS

The Ice Palace

Robert Swindells left school at the age of fifteen and joined the Royal Air Force at seventeen-and-a-half. After his discharge, he worked at a variety of jobs, before training and working as a teacher. He is now a full-time writer and lives with his wife Brenda on the Yorkshire Moors. Robert Swindells has written many books for young people, and in 1984 was the winner of the Children's Book Award and the Other Award for his novel *Brother in the Land*. He won the Children's Book Award for a second time in 1990 with *Room 13*, and in 1994 *Stone Cold* won the Carnegie Medal and the Sheffield Children's Book Award.

ROBERT SWINDELLS

The Ice Palace

Illustrated by June Jackson

PUFFIN BOOKS

PUFFIN BOOKS

Published by the Penguin Group
Penguin Books Ltd, 27 Wrights Lane, London W8 5TZ, England
Penguin Putnam Inc., 375 Hudson Street, New York,
New York 10014, USA
Penguin Books Australia Ltd, Ringwood, Victoria, Australia
Penguin Books Canada Ltd, 10 Alcorn Avenue, Toronto,
Ontario, Canada M4V 3B2
Penguin Books (NZ) Ltd, Private Bag 102902, NSMC,
Auckland, New Zealand

On the worldwide web at: www.penguin.com

Penguin Books Ltd, Registered Offices: Harmondsworth,
Middlesex, England

First published by Hamish Hamilton Ltd 1977
Published in Puffin Books 1992
11 13 15 17 19 20 18 16 14 12

Made and printed in England by Clays Ltd, St Ives plc

British Library Cataloguing in Publication Data
A CIP catalogue record for this book is available from
the British Library

ISBN 0-140-34966-9

For Brenda

Turn your face into the east wind, and if you could see for ever you would see Ivan's land. It is a land where summer is short and pale like a celandine; winter long and cold as an icicle. Ivan does not live there now for he grew

5

old long ago, and is gone. But the people of the pine-woods remember him. They remember him all the time, but most of all they remember him in winter because they are not afraid of winter any more. They have no need to be afraid, because of something Ivan did when he was very small.

Ivan and his brother lived in the house of their father the blacksmith, in a village in the shadow of the great, dark forest. The people of the village were poor, but in the summertime they were mostly happy, so that the pale, warm air rang with their laughter and their singing as they worked.

But as the short summers gave

way to autumn their songs became sad songs, and their laughter thin. For they knew that far away to the north, Starjik was greasing the runners of his sled and rounding up his wolves. Starjik! Whisper his name and it was winter in your heart. Hissing over crisp snow in the black of night came Starjik behind his hungry team. Their eyes were yellow and their fangs

were white. When Starjik was in a village the people lay very still behind their shutters but always, in the morning, a child was gone. For Starjik was known in every pine-woods village as the child-taker, and those he took were never seen again.

One night when an icy wind whined through the black trees, and powdery snow sifted under everybody's doors, Starjik came to Ivan's house, and when Ivan awoke in the morning his little brother was gone.

All the village wept for the blacksmith and his wife, and for little Ivan who must now play alone. And little Ivan walked in Starjik's sled-tracks to the end of

the village and stood there a long time, gazing into the north.

That evening, at suppertime, while his mother and father were not looking, Ivan took some of the dark bread from the big wooden board on the table, and slipped it into his pocket. Then he said, "Mother, I am very tired. I will sleep now." His mother lighted a candle for him and he carried the little flame into his room.

For a long time he sat on his bed, listening to the small noises his parents made beyond the door of his room, and to the wind outside. The wind made a sad, lonely sound, and as he listened it seemed to Ivan that something was crying out there in the night; something

small and frightened that touched his window and moved away along the wall. And he lifted a corner of the window-curtain and pressed his face to the cold glass and whispered, "Wait, little brother. I will not leave you. I am coming." His breath made a cloud on the glass, and there was only the wind. He let the curtain fall, blew out his candle, and climbed into bed without taking off his clothes.

After a while, the door of his room was opened quietly and Ivan pretended to be sleeping while his mother smoothed his quilt, kissed him and went out, closing the door behind her. Soon after that the unhappy couple went to their room and the house was still.

Ivan slipped out of bed and pulled on his boots. Then he took his fur parka and moved quietly to the door. Moments later he was across the warm, dark kitchen and out into the freezing wind.

Next morning the people were awakened by a terrible cry from the blacksmith's house. The blacksmith's wife had crept early into Ivan's room and found his bed empty. All that day the people stood about the village in groups, talking, but nobody had heard Starjik come again, and nobody could remember having known anyone as unlucky as the blacksmith and his wife.

And far away, through the

forest and over the hill walked Ivan. He wore his fur parka, and between his teeth he held a squirrel-tail, for if he had not, the wind would have frozen his breath into a mask of ice on his face.

Ivan was afraid. He was more afraid than he had ever been, for nobody had ever seen Starjik's

land, and lived to return home.
His head was bowed and he cried a
little as he went along, and his
tears became pips of ice before
they touched the snow. He was

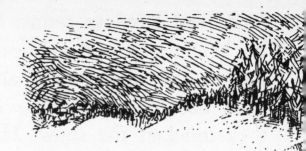

afraid, and sometimes he almost
turned around, to follow his footprints back to his father's house.
But then he would see in his mind a
picture of his brother, holding out
his arms and crying, in a place that
was cold beyond imagining. And
then Ivan would brush away his
tears and go on.

On and on he went, and when it
began to grow dark he found a
snowdrift and tunnelled into it as

18

his father had taught him. Outside, the screaming wind drove blizzards of snow across the darkness, but Ivan slept safe and warm in his shelter. When morning came he dug himself out, ate a little food from his pocket and looked all around. His footprints were gone and the wind had shifted the snowdrifts into a new pattern so that he could not tell which way he had come. He sighed, turned his face into the wind, and walked on.

The snow was deeper now, and Ivan's feet sank far beneath its surface with every step. He began to feel tired, and to wonder if he would ever see his home again. He was thinking longingly about his chair by the big, hot stove, when there came a sound that felt like an icicle in his heart. It was the long, thin cry a hungry wolf makes when it scents its prey. The cry was answered by another, and soon the pinewood echoed with the howls of the hunting pack.

Ivan tried to go faster but the snow sucked at his boots, making him stumble. He looked back, sobbing. His footprints wound away between the trees, and somewhere back there, he knew, the wolves were running in his tracks with their noses down to smell him out.

A tree: he must find a tree to climb. Wolves can outrun any living thing but they cannot climb trees. He stumbled on, looking wildly around him, but the trees just here were all pines with smooth, icy trunks. The wolf-cries drew nearer. He looked back. Dim shapes moved in the dark beneath the trees. He plunged forward, gasping. They had seen him now. A few seconds more and they would be upon him. He glanced all about and ploughed through the snow, the wolves at his heels. He leapt; his hands closed around the lowest branch and he swung his legs clear of the ground as the first wolf lunged in a flurry of snow.

Painfully, Ivan hauled himself up into the ice-lacquered branches and sat, gazing down. The wolves milled, snarling, around the foot of the tree. Their slavering jaws were upturned and their breath rose in plumes around him. Now and then a wolf would leap, its jaws snapping within inches of his feet.

Soon, Ivan began to feel cold. The wind whipped through the bare branches and his dangling legs became numb. Soon he knew the frost would be in his fingers. It would spread through his hands until they could no longer grip, and he would fall into that whirling mass of fur and fangs. "Go away!" he cried. "Oh go away and find something else to kill!" But the wolves gazed at him with their cruel eyes and their jaws seemed to grin. "They know," sobbed Ivan. "They know that I am freezing.

They're waiting for me to fall."

He clung desperately to his perch. The cold began to seep through his hands. He cried softly, and his tears froze on his cheeks. "Farewell little brother," he whispered. "I can never save you now." His eyes felt heavy, and his head sank slowly until his chin rested on his chest. He was going to

sleep. The cold was going away. He smiled a little. He had only to let go now, and he could sleep and sleep until the end of the world . . .

A startled yelp roused him. He shook his head and looked down. The wolves were scattering in all directions and in their midst, rearing on its hind legs, was a huge bear. Its terrible claws hissed through the air and the wolves fell back, snapping. The bear lunged at them and they turned tail, slipping away between the frozen trees.

Ivan cried out joyfully, then gaped with horror. Bears kill people. And bears can climb! He pulled up his feet, trying to move higher. The bear dropped on to all its four feet and stood a moment, snarling into the forest. Then, with only an upward glance at the boy, it loped off, melting soon among the shadows of the pines.

Stiffly, Ivan climbed down. He peered fearfully all around but the wolves were gone, and there was no sign of the bear.

All that day little Ivan walked on. Now and then he would break off a little of the bread in his pocket and chew it as he walked. And when it began to grow dark he found another snowdrift and made a cave inside it. He ate more of the bread and snuggled down to sleep.

At midnight he awoke, and it seemed to him that he had heard a voice. He listened. Outside the wind was howling. After a moment he closed his eyes again. "It must have been the wind," he said to himself. "Only the wind." But no sooner had he closed his eyes than he seemed to hear the voice again. He got up, knelt by the hole, and stuck his head out. The cold made him gasp. Ivan screwed up his eyes and peered into the darkness. There was nothing. Only the tossing of the pines and clouds of windblown snow. Then, just as he was about to draw his head back inside, he thought he saw a movement under the trees. A small figure flitting across a paler patch between the shadows. Ivan cried out, clambering from the

snowdrift. The figure; it seemed impossible, but from here it had looked like—"Little brother!" he cried. "Wait!"

He was stumbling through deep snow. As he drew near, the small figure seemed to move back, so that he was always the same distance away from it. "Wait!" he cried again, "oh don't run away. It is Ivan, come to take you home." But the figure was only a smudge now; a shadow in the shadows, and as he watched it faded and was gone. And he heard laughter in the wind and whirled

around, but no-one was there.

The cold was like knives in his feet and he looked down at himself through his tears. "My boots!" he gasped. "I left them in the snow-drift, and my mittens too." He turned. "I must go back at once or

I will die!" He knew now that the figure in the trees had been Starjik's cruel trick, and the laughter in the wind Starjik's laughter. But when he looked around, he could not tell which way he had come. He ran, first this way, then that; stumbling in the snow but no way seemed to be the right way. The voice laughed more loudly in the wind.

Ivan stopped. He was lost, and knew that very soon he would fall into a sleep from which he would never awaken. He closed his eyes, and was about to sink down on the snow when he heard a shrill scream. He jerked his head round and saw a white shape that flew soundlessly between the trees. As

he watched, it settled on a branch and stared at him with great yellow eyes. "Go away, snowy-owl," he whispered. "Go away and find a mouse to eat. I am no use to you. I am no use to anyone."

The owl leapt from its perch with a scream, circled his head on velvet wings, and made off through the forest. After a moment it came back and flew round his head again. "Perhaps," thought Ivan, "it wants me to follow it." He was becoming very weary, but when the great white bird flew away again he followed. In a few moments he saw the snowdrift in which he had made his shelter. He fell to his knees by the entrance and crawled inside

34

with the last of his strength. The snowy-owl circled the snowdrift once and was gone.

When dawn came, Ivan wrapped himself up in his warm clothing and set out again. There was only a little bread left now in his pocket and he knew he must save it, for he still had far to go.

The wind was strong and the snow was deep, and Ivan went very slowly, with his head down. All at once he felt the snow shift, and he cried out. Beneath his feet a great crack opened up, and lumps of snow as big as houses fell into it with a hissing roar. He flung himself forward, trying to reach the other side. His mittens grabbed at the lip of the crack but it

crumbled and he was falling. Desperately he clutched at a tiny fir tree that grew outward from the side of the crack. It was so small that he knew it would never hold him; his weight would pull it out by the root and he would fall, down, down with the tumbling snow-blocks to be buried for ever in the bottom of the crack.

But the little fir tree held. It jerked him to a stop, and held. And he dangled by one arm over the drop as an avalanche of snow hurtled roaring into the chasm.

Afterwards, he could never tell how long he hung there. He only knew that at last the avalanche stopped, and he scrambled his way somehow out of that ghastly crack.

For a long time he lay in the snow, sobbing with fright at the horrible fate he had escaped. Then, wearily, he got to his feet and brushed the snow from his clothes with his mittened hands. His heart was heavy, and if it had not been for the crack that now blocked the way, he might have given up and returned to his distant home. As it was he sighed, turned his face into the north wind, and went on.

Presently it began to grow dark. "I must find another snowdrift," said Ivan to himself. He sighed. Long ago, when his father had taught him how to make a snowden, it had been fun. Now it just seemed like hard work. "Snowdens are quite warm," he thought,

38

"but they are not like my little bed at home." The sky was a deep grey, turning black, when Ivan found his snowdrift. He fell to his knees and began to scrape out a tunnel with his mittened hands.

After a moment he stopped, his head tilted to one side. From far away, carried on the wind, he thought he heard music. He listened. The pine trees creaked and sighed, and snow-powder hissed over the frosty crust. Then he heard it again. It was the sound of a fiddle. Ivan screwed up his eyes and shook his head fiercely. No! It was not real. It could not be real. It was another cruel trick to hurt him, to keep him from doing what he must do. He began once more to scrape at the snow, whistling a little between his teeth to blot out the sound of the fiddle. But when he stopped, there it was, rising and falling in the wind. He got to his feet and gazed towards the sound, biting his lip. There was a faint glow in the sky beyond the pines. And now he was sure there were voices too, mixed in with the fiddle. He looked down at his unfinished den, then out again towards the glow. It *seemed* real; all of it. The fiddle, the voices, and the glow. He saw a picture in his mind of people; happy people who laughed and shouted and danced to a fiddle, and suddenly he was overcome with loneliness. He left the snowdrift and began hurrying

through the trees, his eyes fixed on that warm, hypnotic glow.

He came out of the trees on to a long slope and there below him lay a village. Lamplight glowed warmly in all its windows and spilled out of open doorways on to a crowded street. Everyone in the village seemed to be out of doors and when Ivan looked down the street he could see why. At the far end of it someone had built an enormous fire. Its flames rose high in the air and the snow all round was pink with its glow.

And the music! It wafted in great clouds up the slope and Ivan had never heard such music. He was weary but he wanted to dance. He was far from his home yet he felt like shouting. And up towards him, their laughter spangling the night came children; a long ribbon of children hand-in-hand, running up the hill. When they drew near they stopped, and their leader smiled, holding out his hand to Ivan. "Come," he said. "Tonight is a feast, and you are welcome here." And though it was winter, and though the night was a cold one, these children had on summer clothes, and all the girls wore flowers in their hair.

In the village below the fiddles began a fresh tune. The line of children stirred, restlessly, like a string of spirited ponies. The boy beckoned, his smile inviting. "Come," he said once more. "My

43

friends would dance." And step-
ping forward, Ivan slipped off a
mitten and gave his hand. At once
they went whirling away, across
the slopes and down; down to
where the people danced through
pools of lamplight on the snow.
Ivan, skipping, threw back his

44

head and laughed. The line had reversed itself so that now the last child had become the first and was leading them on to the street.

Once in the village they did not keep to the street, but began threading themselves like a many-coloured serpent to and fro between the houses. Once their leader took them through the doorway of a house, and Ivan had a glimpse of tables, chairs and a big tiled stove before he was whirled out again into the night. People were everywhere, but if anyone noticed the stranger in their midst, no-one seemed to mind.

The music grew louder, and coming round the corner of a

house, Ivan saw that they were close to the great fire. In the flames an ox was roasting and nearby, on upturned barrels, sat the fiddlers. Their bows flashed back and forth across the strings of their fiddles, and they tapped their feet in time upon the beaten snow.

The line of children circled, forming a ring with the fiddlers in the middle. Round and round they whirled, the firelight dancing in their eyes. Then the circle broke, and the child who had led them was thrust into the centre, among the fiddlers, and the tune changed, and she danced a special dance for them while they went round and round. When her dance was finished the girl rejoined the circle, the next child was pushed forward and the tune changed again. Ivan watched through tears of joy. The cold was gone, and the loneliness. What would be the tune, when *his* turn came, and what steps would he dance?

Round, and round, and round. The people of the village had stopped their dancing now, and were crowding forward to watch the children. And as they watched, they clapped their hands to the fast, clever rhythm.

The boy beside Ivan grinned, winked at him, and leapt into the centre. The child whose dance was done took Ivan's hand. The circle never stopped spinning. "My dance next!" cried Ivan. "A few more moments, and *I* will show you dancing!"

They whirled on; Ivan gasped as a volley of wind whipped about his legs, unimaginably cold. It scooped up a twist of crystals and spun them about his body. In an instant he was blinded as the stinging powder lashed his eyes. He tore his hands from those of his friends and fell to the ground, clawing at his face.

The crystals turned to water and he blinked them from his eyes. He had broken the circle; he must get up and take his place or the dance would be spoiled. Already the fiddlers had stopped playing . . .

He scrambled to his knees and cried out in pain and disbelief. The fire was gone. There was no ring of children, nor any mark upon the snow where they had been. There were no villagers. The houses lay cold and broken along the empty street. Snow sifted through sagging doors and the wind moaned in sightless windows, stirring here and there a rag of ancient curtain.

He knelt there in the snow and wept for the pretty phantoms of the dance; his tears becoming ice upon his cheek. And when at last the crying stopped, so that he could see again, he saw before him a great black hole in the place where the fiddlers had been. A well: a deep, deep well with smooth sides and black, icy water far down in the bottom of it. And he knew that if his turn had come to dance, then that black water would have closed for ever over his head.

He got to his feet, shuddering; backing away from the well. Was

it possible? They had been so beautiful; they had befriended him and made him one of them. Would they have led him to the brink of the well? Would they have let him fall? He stood there; forlorn in the broken village. The wind blew round him and there was laughter in it, and he knew.

He turned and ran, along the silent street that had no footprint on it but his own. Past the last house and out on to the moon-washed slope. His feet sank into the snow and his lungs were bursting, but he did not stop until he topped the slope and plunged deep among the black pines. There he found a snowdrift, burrowed into it, and cried softly till sleep came.

He set out the next morning, weary and sad. He felt even more lonely than before. It seemed to him that he had no friend in the world. There were only enemies out here in the wilderness. His bread was almost gone. There was one piece left but he dared not eat it, for he did not know how much further he had to go.

He had not walked far when, turning to look back, he saw something moving, far away between the snow-laden trees. At first it looked like a whirl of snow crystals whipped by the wind, but as it came closer he saw that it was an old woman in a grey sparkling shawl which flapped about her as she came. He waited. The old

woman came slowly, bending down now and then to pick something from the snow. When she came near she straightened up, gazing at Ivan. Strands of her hair whipped across her face like sleet, but she was smiling.

Ivan took off his mitten, put his hand into his pocket and pulled out a crust of bread. He held it out to her. "Old woman," he said "it is cold, and you must be very far from your home. Share my bread. It will warm you a little, perhaps."

The old woman shook her head. "You are kind," she said gently, "but I do not need your bread."

Ivan did not understand. "Old woman," he said, "what did you do when it was night and the wind howled like a hungry wolf?"

The old woman smiled. "You are a good boy to care about an old woman like me. But I am not an old woman always. Sometimes I am an icicle, or a bear, or a spruce-tree. Sometimes I am a twist of windblown snow, colder than the night." Her eyes twinkled at him. "One night," she said, "I was a snowy-owl."

Ivan stared, remembering how he had been lost and freezing in the night. "Were you," he said, "the owl who showed me the way? And the bear who drove off the wolves? And the little fir tree in the crack?"

The old woman smiled. "It may well be so," she said, "for lovers find small miracles, no matter what men say, and no-one ever loved better than you love your brother."

"How do you know of this?" cried Ivan, "and what do you pick from the snow?"

The old woman held out her hand to him. Pips of ice lay like diamonds in her palm. "These are the tears that you cried for your brother," she said. "I have followed you, gathering them from the snow because you will need them soon."

Ivan frowned. "What would I do with tears?" he said. "Why will I need them soon?"

"To soften Starjik's heart," replied the old woman. "Here, take them." And she tipped the icy pips into Ivan's hand.

Ivan gazed at them. "I do not understand," he said. "What am I to do with these tears?"

The old woman became grave. "At the moment of your greatest

danger," she said, "you must fling the tears into Starjik's face and say:

"Brothers never more shall part
Melt the winter in his heart."

Ivan said the words softly to himself so that he would remember, and the old woman nodded. "That is right," she said. "And now go, for I can help you no more."

When he had gone a little way, Ivan turned to wave farewell but there was only a little spruce-tree that quivered in the wind. He turned and walked on, and after a long time he came to a mountain. It was a hard, white mountain and as he drew near the air grew colder still. At the foot of the mountain

was a great high cave with the wind booming in its mouth. Ivan shuddered, because he knew that he had come at last to Starjik's land.

Inside the cave it was utterly black. The roar of the wind was deafening, and it was deadly cold. Ivan stopped. The darkness filled him with dread. He looked back to where the grey light spilled a little way into the entrance. He could go no farther; must get outside where he could see the sky and the snow and the trees. But his brother must have passed this way. Somewhere in this terrible place the little boy was waiting; waiting for Ivan to come and take him home. He set his lips in a thin, firm line and moved on into the blackness, holding out his arms before him and going very slowly. The wind howled in his ears and he heard again the laughing voice in it. Something fluttered in his face. He struck at it with his hand and it slid up over his forehead and became tangled in his parka, dragging the hood from his head. At once something else hit him, flapping coldly in his hair. Ivan cried out, clawing the thing from his head. It sank needle-teeth into his finger and whirled away on the wind.

Another one, this time on his chest. He threw up his arms to protect his face.

Whatever the things were, they

64

were all around him. He felt the small collisions, felt them cling, fluttering to his clothing. He screamed, but the wind drowned the cry. He whirled round and round, beating at himself to knock them off, and for every one he brushed away there was another one to take its place.

He knew that it was hopeless. He put his head down, wrapped his arms around it and went through them, and after a time the collisions stopped.

For a long time Ivan moved onward through the cold darkness. The sound of the wind began to fade and when he looked back he could no longer see the light.

As he walked he noticed that the

tunnel was becoming higher and wider, and he seemed to be moving towards a lighted place. Presently he stopped, listening intently. Somewhere in front of him he heard a laugh. It was not a pleasant laugh, like the laugh of someone who is enjoying a good joke. It was a cold, flat laugh, and when it came again Ivan found himself thinking about the laughter he had heard in the wind, last night when he was lost and freezing.

As he moved on the laughter grew louder and he could hear other sounds too; a swishing noise, and now and then a thin, high scream.

The tunnel, which by now was

wide and very high, took a sudden turn. The sounds seemed to be coming from just beyond the turn. Ivan flattened himself against the wall, peered cautiously round, and almost cried out.

He was looking into a great, glittering cavern. The floor was blue ice and enormous icicles hung in thousands from the roof. Hard blue light glowed and flickered like cold fire and the wind from the passage moaned around the walls.

In the centre of the cavern, its back towards the boy, stood a hideous figure. It was stooped and crooked, and its white robe hung in folds from a bony frame. In one hand it gripped a thin, springy rod, of the kind which Ivan's people used to fish for trout in the river. As Ivan watched, the figure turned, pulling on the rod and watching something that fluttered and squealed far up near the roof, among the icicles.

It was then that Ivan saw what the man was doing, and his heart turned cold. Fishing! The creature was fishing, but not in the water, and not for fish. He was fishing in the air, and his victim was a tiny bat that whirled and tugged frantically as the man began to wind in the thin line. But struggle as it might, the poor creature was pulled closer and closer to its monstrous captor, and soon Ivan could see a streak of blood at its mouth from the cruel hook. When

the terrified creature was close
enough, the man clawed it out of
the air, crushed it and dropped it
on to the ice, where the broken
bodies of several others lay. Then
he threw back his head and
laughed horribly.

Ivan drew back into the passage. The man's cruelty had sickened him, and the laughter turned his blood cold. He tried to tell himself that it didn't matter. The man had not seen him, so he could just turn round and run away and never see the creature again.

But deep within himself he knew the name of this monster. No other man could possibly behave with such cruelty. This man was Starjik and Ivan knew that if he fell into those awful hands, he need expect no more mercy than the poor, broken bat. And somewhere not far away, this creature had his brother.

The thought of his little brother in the hands of such a man filled

Ivan with rage. He was so angry that his fear left him. He would fling himself on Starjik, snatch the rod from his hand and beat him with it until he screamed like the bat had screamed. He clenched his fists and stepped into the open.

Instantly he froze. It was as though his arms and legs had become ice. Try as he might, he could not move.

Starjik no longer fished. He sat now in the middle of the cavern, on a throne of age-grey wood, and his icy stare held Ivan rigid. He moved a hand; beckoning with one grey finger. The pale eyes now seemed to draw Ivan across the icy floor until he stood trembling before the throne. Starjik stared

down at him, his hands gripping the arms of the chair. His grey beard was stiff with ice and his hair fell in frozen strands about his thin shoulders. After a long time he spoke, and his voice was like walking on crisp snow.

"Who are you?"

Ivan stood up very straight. He hoped that Starjik could not see him trembling. "I am Ivan," he said. "The blacksmith is my father."

Starjik's lips twitched cruelly. "Why do you come here?" he hissed. "Do you not know that all who enter Starjik's land are dead?"

"I have come for my brother," said Ivan.

"Your brother is dead," said Starjik. Ivan shook his head.

"No, he is not dead, I can feel him, in here." He touched his chest with a mittened hand.

"That is not possible!" snapped Starjik. "People cannot *feel* other people. They can only *see* them or *hear* them!" He flung out a hand. "Do you *see* your brother here? Do you *hear* him?"

Ivan shook his head. "No. But he is nearby."

Starjik gripped the arm of his throne and rose to his feet. "Very well," he said, softly. "You are right, little Ivan, your brother *is* close by." He turned, beckoning. "Come, and I will show you."

Ivan's heart leapt. He did not

see the smile on Starjik's lips as he turned and shuffled across the floor. Ivan followed.

To one side of the cavern an ice-curtain hung from roof to floor. Starjik went behind this curtain and Ivan was close on his heels. The man turned with a leer, pointing. "Well, Ivan, here he is. Was it worth all the hardships of your journey?"

Ivan clapped a hand to his mouth, stifling a cry. He was looking at a great block of ice. It was higher than three houses and as long as the cavern. The ice was as clear as a crystal pool and inside he saw children. Many children, trapped in the solid ice. Some looked as though they had been

running, others seemed to have been skipping. Some sat and some stood. There were frozen smiles and frozen frowns, and there, right at the front, gazing out from his icy prison, was Ivan's brother.

Starjik laughed cruelly. "Such pretty children," he said, "and mine, for ever."

Ivan looked into the twisted face and his eyes were filled with tears. "But these children do not move," he cried. "You cannot play with them or hear them laugh. You could make such children from painted wood."

Starjik shook his head. "Ah no! The finest wood-carver could not do that. And besides, I take the children to punish those who sent me away." He laughed again. "Once I was a child like these," he said "but the other children would not play with me. They said my heart was cold, and they sent me away."

He turned to the ice-prison, resting his hands on it, looking in. "Now I have friends, and every one a pretty one, for I have chosen them myself." He turned, smiling coldly down at Ivan. "You, also, are a pretty child," he hissed. "You would not be out of place in my collection, you would not be out of place at all. They are happy, you know, with me, for they have forgotten their homes. And now it is time for you to join them." H reached up and sn-

Discussion + writing to a character

from the curtain. Ivan backed away. Starjik laughed. "It is no use, Ivan. You cannot escape. I have only to touch you with this icicle and you are mine for ever."

Ivan felt the ice-prison at his back. He could go no further. Starjik grinned and came on, the icicle held out before him. Ivan bit his lip. The ice-point was inches from his head. As Starjik stooped for the final lunge the boy whipped off his mitten and flung the ice-pips into the evil face. His voice echoed shrill through the cavern:

"Brothers never more shall part:
Melt the winter in his heart!"

At once there came a rumbling sound and the cavern floor quivered. Starjik staggered back with

an awful cry, his hands clawing at his face. Ivan was flung to the floor. Behind him, the ice-prison heaved, split, and shivered into fragments. He scrabbled at the slippery floor, trying to get up. Then something struck him on the head and he felt himself falling, falling . . .

After a long time Ivan opened his eyes, and cried out. Starjik was bending over him. He rolled away, trying to get up. Starjik watched him. Ivan scrambled to his feet and backed off, eyeing the old man warily. Starjik made no attempt to follow, but stood, gazing at him across the shattered ice. Then the corner of his mouth twitched, so that he seemed almost to smile.

Ivan screwed up his eyes, shook his head, and looked again. Starjik *was* smiling. There was no cruelty now in his smile. There was something in his hand, and he held it out towards Ivan. "Soup," he said, "hot soup."

Ivan took a step forward. Something grabbed at his waist and clung there, very tightly. He looked down and saw his brother's head pressed against him. All around children were awakening; rubbing their eyes and gazing about them. Starjik came closer, offering the soup. He seemed straighter now; less twisted. Ivan took the bowl and backed away, drinking the hot soup and watching Starjik through the steam.

"There are furs," said Starjik. "In my store-room; many furs. I will fetch them." He shuffled away through the splintered ice. Ivan gazed after him, wonderingly, passing the soup-bowl to his brother.

Starjik went several times back and forth with his shuffling gait until a heap of warm furs lay on the floor. "You ought to be going," he said. "There is no wind now and you have a long journey." And he began to go round from child to child, wrapping the furs about their shoulders; smiling. And when they began to move out through the passage in twos, holding hands behind Ivan, Starjik led the way. There was no wind, and

no fluttering things now in the quiet darkness, and they came at last to the end of the cave, where their eyes danced to see the snow-flakes falling through the pure light.

"You will never see me again," said Starjik, "but I shall see you. And when winter comes again you will have reason to remember how Starjik's heart was warmed."

And so they left Starjik's land, and Ivan took them home. And at every village he strode along the street crying, "Here are your children, home again from far away!" And the people cheered, and brought food, and heaped gifts upon them, and stood waving as the line of children marched away. With each village the line became a little shorter, until at last only Ivan and his brother were left.

And so they came home. And the fear melted in the hearts of the people and they were happy.

And when winter came again, Starjik remembered his promise. No-one heard him come, for the howling wolves were gone and his

sled was pulled now by silent deer.
But when the people woke at dawn
there were sled-tracks in the snow,
and shining gifts by all the
children's beds.

URSULA BEAR

Sheila Lavelle

Pretending to be a bear is fun, but it's not the same as *being* a bear.

Ursula's dream comes true when she discovers a book of magic spells in the library and turns herself into a bear.

But she completely forgets to read how she can change herself back into a little girl again!

Two delightful stories about Ursula Bear together for the first time in one volume.

READ MORE IN PUFFIN

For children of all ages, Puffin represents quality and variety – the very best in publishing today around the world.

For complete information about books available from Puffin – and Penguin – and how to order them, contact us at the appropriate address below. Please note that for copyright reasons the selection of books varies from country to country.

On the worldwide web: www.puffin.co.uk

In the United Kingdom: Please write to *Dept. EP, Penguin Books Ltd, Bath Road, Harmondsworth, West Drayton, Middlesex UB7 0DA*

In the United States: Please write to *Consumer Sales, Penguin USA, P.O. Box 999, Dept. 17109, Bergenfield, New Jersey 07621-0120.* VISA and MasterCard holders call 1-800-253-6476 to order Penguin titles

In Canada: Please write to *Penguin Books Canada Ltd, 10 Alcorn Avenue, Suite 300, Toronto, Ontario M4V 3B2*

In Australia: Please write to *Penguin Books Australia Ltd, P.O. Box 257, Ringwood, Victoria 3134*

In New Zealand: Please write to *Penguin Books (NZ) Ltd, Private Bag 102902, North Shore Mail Centre, Auckland 10*

In India: Please write to *Penguin Books India Pvt Ltd, 706 Eros Apartments, 56 Nehru Place, New Delhi 110 019*

In the Netherlands: Please write to *Penguin Books Netherlands bv, Postbus 3507, NL-1001 AH Amsterdam*

In Germany: Please write to *Penguin Books Deutschland GmbH, Metzlerstrasse 26, 60594 Frankfurt am Main*

In Spain: Please write to *Penguin Books S. A., Bravo Murillo 19, 1° B, 28015 Madrid*

In Italy: Please write to *Penguin Italia s.r.l., Via Felice Casati 20, I–20124 Milano.*

In France: Please write to *Penguin France S. A., 17 rue Lejeune, F–31000 Toulouse*

In Japan: Please write to *Penguin Books Japan, Ishikiribashi Building, 2–5–4, Suido, Bunkyo-ku, Tokyo 112*

In South Africa: Please write to *Longman Penguin Southern Africa (Pty) Ltd, Private Bag X08, Bertsham 2013*